A CHRISTMAS SONATA

YEARLING BOOKS are designed especially to entertain and enlighten young people. Patricia Reilly Giff, consultant to this series, received her bachelor's degree from Marymount College and a master's degree in history from St. John's University. She holds a Professional Diploma in Reading and a Doctorate of Humane Letters from Hofstra University. She was a teacher and reading consultant for many years, and is the author of numerous books for young readers.

A CHRISTMAS SONATA

BY GARY PAULSEN

Illustrated by Leslie Bowman

A YEARLING BOOK

Published by
Bantam Doubleday Dell Books for Young Readers
a division of
Bantam Doubleday Dell Publishing Group, Inc.
1540 Broadway
New York, New York 10036

ISBN 0-440-40958-6

Reprinted by arrangement with Delacorte Press

Printed in the United States of America

October 1994

10   9   8   7

For my mother's laughter

A CHRISTMAS SONATA

*I*t comes on every-
body at a certain time in their life to not
believe in Santa Claus.

For me it came during the war, the
Second World War, and my father was fighting in Europe. We lived in a large, poor
apartment in Minneapolis for a time then,
and my mother worked in a laundry during
the day and could not always be with me.

Different people on our floor took care
of me at different times, or were supposed

to, but often I just had the run of the floor. I was probably a nuisance and yet most people were more than nice to me. I would sometimes spend whole days in different apartments, eating cookies and listening to the radio or playing war with a small wooden gun that I had and everybody seemed to tolerate me.

But there was one old man named Henderson, who lived with his wife at the end of our floor, who did not like children. He did not like me in particular, but I thought he must not like any children and a week before Christmas in 1943 I was playing in the hall, running back and forth, when I passed Henderson's apartment and saw something that stopped me cold.

Mr. Henderson was standing by the kitchen table with his wife. On the table was a glass jar of red wine. I knew about red wine because one of my baby-sitters was an old woman who drank red wine from a jar.

Mr. Henderson had some wine in a jelly glass and just as I ran past he was taking a drink.

He was dressed in a Santa Claus suit.

There were too many things to take in, too many stunning things. I had complete, utter belief in Santa Claus. I had seen him in a store sitting on a raised platform, had been terrified by his power over me. I tried to be good; and when it didn't work and I was bad I hoped that he would not hear of it, and when I sat in his lap to tell him what I wanted I nearly peed in fear. He meant Christmas and toys and more to me and I had seen his work. The year before I had asked for an army rifle with a wooden bullet that moved back and forth with the bolt and Santa did not find out that I had played with matches and I found the rifle beneath the tree on Christmas morning.

And now I found that Santa Claus was Mr. Henderson. An old man who drank red wine and scratched and spit and swore at me, and who I had heard my mother say to a neighbor woman couldn't hold a job—that was Santa Claus.

I could not believe it and so I stood in his open door and looked up at him and asked him:

"Are you Santa Claus?"

He looked down at me and took a drink of wine and nodded. "Sure, kid. I'm Santa Claus."

I believed him. He had no reason to lie to me and he was standing there in the suit with the hat on and his wife was holding his beard. How could he not be Santa Claus?

I ran back to our apartment and cried some. When mother came home from work she had a can of Spam, which we ate at dinner with fried potatoes, but even that was not good enough to cheer me and I told her.

"Mr. Henderson is Santa Claus."

Mother stopped chewing. "What do you mean?"

"I saw him today. He was dressed in his suit and I asked him if he was Santa Claus and he said he was."

She didn't say anything.

"I thought Santa Claus lived at the North Pole and had reindeer, and now Mr. Henderson says he's him. Is that right?"

"Not really, punkin. Sometimes stores will hire somebody at Christmas to pretend he is Santa Claus so that children can talk to him—"

"But there is only supposed to be one Santa Claus, isn't there?"

"Yes, but . . ."

And of course it didn't matter after that, didn't matter what she said. It was done. Santa Claus was ruined, was gone, and I knew he didn't exist and that I had been lied to and there had never been a Santa Claus.

I cried some and Mother sat with me for a time on the couch that felt like a carpet and had flowers on it, and she said some things about Mr. Henderson that weren't very nice. But it didn't change what I had seen or knew and I would probably have spent the rest of my childhood and perhaps my whole life not believing in Santa Claus.

But the next day mother came home from work and sat at the kitchen table. She put me in her lap and opened an envelope.

"We got a letter today from Marilyn. She wants us to come up and spend Christmas with them at the store in Winnipah. You'll get to see Matthew and everything. Won't that be fun?"

I had mixed feelings about going north. My uncle Ben and aunt Marilyn owned a store in the town of Winnipah. The store was right on the lake, with a dock that went out over the water. I had only been there in the summer, when we lay on the dock and watched the large green fish swim down in the cool shadows.

I had never seen it in the winter and didn't think it would be as much fun as it had been in the summer.

And Matthew was a problem as well. He had something wrong with him so that everybody said he was dying. I wasn't supposed to know it, but I had heard the grown-ups talking about it more than once, sitting and crying and talking about it. Dying didn't mean the things to me then that it did later. All I really knew was that Matthew had to stay in a bed in the back room of the store and was all puffy and yellow-looking. Dying to me meant what Mother worried about all the time—that Father would die in Europe and not come home. I did not think of it as an end so much as somebody just not coming home, and had not worked out how Matthew could die when he was already home.

And then there was Santa Claus. When you are young it is necessary to be more practical than it is when the years have you. I was convinced that there was not a Santa Claus, but what if I was wrong? Would he be able to find us if we were not home?

This was, of course, a crucial issue, as well as the fact that if indeed Santa Claus *was* Mr. Henderson, I only had about a week to be nice to him and get him to like me. Judging by the way he treated me it would be a difficult job, and so when Mother said how much fun it would be to visit Uncle Ben for Christmas there were too many factors involved to give a quick answer.

I thought about it and thought about it and was still thinking about it when Mother dressed me in my coat and snowsuit so I looked like a blue marshmallow, and we rode the bus down to the train station two days later.

I loved trains. They were like huge, friendly monsters, and in the station Mother took me close to the engine so I could look at it. The wheels seemed to reach to the ceiling, and even though there was an engineer up in the little cabin, I did not think trains were run by people. I thought they were alive somehow and carried us because they liked us and were just resting in the station, letting out puffs of steam and rumbling, and that the engineers were just there to take care of things and feed the engine.

It was morning when we left, and the car was warm and had soft seats. Mother took off all my winter clothes and put them in the racks over the seats and let me sit next to the window.

The glass had frost all around but was clear in the middle, and it was like looking through a telescope at the world. People came and went, and on another platform I

saw a soldier come off a train and run to meet a woman who almost jumped on him and hugged him. When I turned to Mother, she had seen it as well and was crying.

"Aren't they lucky to be together for Christmas?" She wiped her eyes and pushed my hair out of my face. "I miss your father, punkin. So much."

I was going to tell her that it wouldn't be so bad because we were going to the store, and she liked to be with Aunt Marilyn because they laughed together all the time, but before I could speak the train jerked.

And jerked again.

And then it started to roll out of the station, and I had my eyes on the window and couldn't think of speaking.

It started slowly, but in a few minutes it was going so fast that the city seemed to stream past the window like running water. I would look ahead and try to see something, catch it as it went by and try to see what it was, but I couldn't. There were backsides of buildings with signs on them, and warehouses with pictures on the side showing big smiling faces and letters as big as houses, but I couldn't see any of them— everything moved so fast it was all a blur and then the city was gone.

Gone. We were out in the country and everything slowed down into rolling hills covered with snow. There were trees, but no leaves, and I could not remember seeing anything so white and clean. Winter in the city was gray and the snow was dirty, but out here it was so bright it hurt my eyes and I had to turn away.

"Isn't it pretty, punkin?" Mother smiled, the tears gone. "Christmas in the country is always prettier."

We went faster and faster, the train wheels clacking. I did not know or understand time then, but I heard the conductor tell Mother it would take eight hours and I knew that Mother worked eight hours a day at the laundry, so I knew how long that was.

All day.

All day on the train. In a little time I turned away from the window. We sat in a seat in the middle of the car and the car was full of people. Each person had a different face and a different set of eyes and different clothes and I wanted to see them all, each and every one, so I ran up and down the car and tried to look at each one.

Mother stamped her foot and made a face at me and I came back and sat down before I'd finished.

"They're all different," I said to her. "I just wanted to see them—"

"It's rude to stare at people."

"They all smiled at me. And I smiled back."

"Still, it's rude. Stay here now."

So I sat next to her and drew pictures with my fingers on the ice around the edges of the train window until she went to sleep. When her head was back and her eyes closed, I slipped away again and went up and down the car because it was impossible to sit still. I met different people and talked to them. One was a soldier and I asked him if he knew my dad and he got a sad look in his eye that I did not understand and shook his head. Before I could tell him that my dad was tall and had dark, curly hair and was in a place called Europe the conductor came into the car.

He was a large black man who smiled at me and said: "Where are you supposed to be sitting?"

I pointed to my sleeping mother and he shook his head.

"I'll bet she doesn't know you're running around, does she?"

"No. She wouldn't let me run in the

car when she was awake. She said it was rude, but I don't know if it is or not when people smile at you."

"If she doesn't want you to run maybe you'd better sit next to her."

His smile was wider but I knew he was right and there was the thing with Santa Claus again. What if it was Mr. Henderson and he heard I had been bad on the train?

I went back to the seat and sat next to Mother for what seemed like years until I couldn't wait for her to wake up anymore and my eyes closed and I fell asleep.

"Wake up, punkin, it's time to eat."

Mother was shaking my shoulder and when I woke up I found I was stretched out on the seat across from her. I didn't remember her moving me.

"We have to go to the dining car." She stood and led me to the bathrooms at the end of the car, where she let me go into the one the men used, and I felt good because she usually made me go into the other one. When I came out she looked at me.

"Did you wash your hands?"

"Twice."

And it was the truth, too, although it was partly because it was fun to use the little sink and hear the water whoosh out and not because I felt dirty.

The dining car made me want to whisper.

"Everything is so clean and white," I said to Mother as we came in the end of the car. The tables each had a white tablecloth and smooth wooden chairs, and there was a water pitcher in the center of each table with beautiful silver knives and forks and spoons and a napkin so white that it seemed to take light from the snow outside the window and it hurt my eyes.

A man with deep black skin, wearing a bright white coat, came to our table and looked down. He was smiling and had hair the same color as the silverware and he put a little glass vase with a flower in it on the table.

"For good boys," he said. "Are you a good boy?"

His voice was deep and rolling and made me think of the church bells that rang in the Catholic church each Sunday at the end of the block and I nodded even if it wasn't always true.

"Then your table gets a flower."

He asked Mother what we wanted and she looked at the menu and made the face she makes when something costs too much. I did not understand much—or anything—about money then, but knew when something was too expensive from watching her face; but she smiled at me over the top of the menu.

"We would like the special."

I picked up my menu, but, of course, it

didn't make any sense to me because along with money I didn't understand words yet, although I knew all the letters.

The man left and Mother leaned across the table. "The special is liver and onions with mashed potatoes, and before you make that face I'll tell you that I had to do it because it's the cheapest thing on the menu."

But I didn't make a face. It was all so exciting that even liver and onions didn't sound bad and the man brought them on plates with little silver domes on them that he took off with his finger in a hole at the top so the steam rolled out in a cloud and I didn't care what it was—it looked good.

I ate all of it, even the onions and the little roll made like a cross with the small squares of the white stuff that was supposed to be butter, but wasn't, with the tiny pictures of a flower stamped in them, and thought it didn't taste at all like the liver and onions we sometimes had at home. I decided that sometimes how it came changed the taste, and also decided to ask Mother to make train liver and onions instead of city liver and onions when we got back.

After the liver and onions and little rolls and potatoes, Mother ordered me a small bowl of green ice cream that she called sherbet. The green taste stayed with me all the way back to the seats, where we sat for the rest of the day, except for going to the bathroom and running up and down the aisles when Mother took another nap.

We went by many frozen lakes, and they all had little houses on them, and I asked Mother about the small huts out on the ice.

"Those are fish houses. People sit in there with little stoves to keep them warm while they fish."

"All day?"

She nodded. "And sometimes at night too. When it gets very cold and still at night the smoke from the chimneys goes straight up to the moon, and it looks so pretty. I used to love to go fishing with Papa."

Not all the lakes had the small houses, but most of them did. There were many, many lakes and each time I saw the houses, smoke was coming out of the chimneys, only it was blowing around. I couldn't wait until night to see if it really went up to the moon, but by the time it was dark I had put my face against Mother's arm and could not stay awake and missed it. Missed all of it. I spread out on the seat again and slept, the train rolling and clacking, and did not know anything until Mother shook me awake and the train was stopped.

"We're here, punkin," she said, and dressed me in all the warm clothes she had taken off me, so I looked like a blue marsh-mallow again. She took our suitcase and my hand and we moved out the end of the car into the open place between the cars. Then we turned and stepped off the steps outside, where the conductor yelled:

"Wedding Rapids!"

It was very cold. So cold, my nose seemed to stop and not let me get air, and I had to breathe through my mouth as Mother took me by the hand down in front of the depot. I saw Uncle Ben and Aunt Marilyn standing by the door waiting for us.

They both hugged Mother and hugged me and Marilyn took Mother's suitcase and was crying and Mother was crying and Ben picked me up and carried me to his car.

"Thirty below," he said to Mother. "I wasn't sure the car would start. I'll have to drain the radiator when we get to the store." Then he turned to me and smiled, holding me out. "Do you think Santa will be able to get his reindeer going?"

"There isn't a Santa Claus," I said. "I saw Mr. Henderson drinking red wine."

"Ohhhh." Ben shook his head. "Are we so old then that we have outgrown Santa Claus?"

But before I could answer, we came to the car and Mother and I climbed into the backseat.

"I've had to keep her running," Ben said, getting in. "It was hard to do, what with the gas rationing—but I was afraid to let her stop. If the oil stiffened we'd never get her going again."

"Why is the car a girl?" I asked Mother, but she didn't hear me and was too busy talking to Marilyn, leaning over the front seat and laughing, to notice anything else.

It wasn't a long drive to the store, but I fell asleep again. Bundled in my snowsuit

and coat and scarf, which Mother had left on because it was cool in the backseat when I fell asleep, I didn't move except to fall forward when we stopped.

Mother helped me upright and out of the car, and Ben picked me up again and carried me into the store.

It was in a large wooden building made of white boards. The store was downstairs in the front part, and there was a place for living in the back. The store was built right on the edge of a huge lake—Winnipah Lake —and went out over the water on posts. In the summer, part of the lake was under part of the store, and there was a big dock that went out into the lake still farther.

I only got one or two whiffs of icy air through my scarf, then Ben had me in the store along with Mother and Marilyn and our suitcase, with the door shut tight to stop the cold.

There was so much in the store that I

couldn't see it all. It was a large, long room, open all the way, and the ceiling was very high and made of squares with pictures of flowers and things in them.

Down the left side of the store there was a long wooden counter with a glass front, full of all sorts of things—candy and caps and knives and small cards with flowers on them. The rest of the store was all shelves, except for the back, where there was a big black stove with a fat face that looked like a smiling monster on the door blowing smoke. And back in the corner away from the stove was a Christmas tree that went all the way to the ceiling, but it was all dark.

As Ben carried me down the length of the store, I saw all of this the way I saw things out the train window, moving and blurred; and then we were through the store and into the back, where there were rooms for living.

The back was very small and very bright after the dark of the store out front.

There was a room with a couch and a kitchen table. It looked a lot like our apartment in Minneapolis, except that there were two other rooms off to the side. These were bedrooms and one was for Marilyn and Ben and the other was for Matthew.

"Matthew is asleep," Ben whispered. "You can see him in the morning."

Marilyn and Ben pulled the couch out into a bed for Mother and me, and Mother helped me undress and use the bathroom next to Ben and Marilyn's bedroom, which was smaller than the bathroom on the train. We went to bed, all whispering, so as not to wake Matthew. I felt like we were still moving on the train and stayed awake a little trying to make the couch quit moving.

It's easy to miss things in the mornings.

I often sleep and sleep through things, and Mother has to wake me up, but this first morning at Uncle Ben's store I was awake almost as soon as the grown-ups.

Mother got out of bed, and I opened my eyes and it was still dark outside the window over the sink. Ben and Marilyn were up and Marilyn was making oatmeal on the stove and Mother helped her. They put cinnamon in the oatmeal and the smell was somehow part of Christmas the way the store was part of Christmas and the train ride was part of Christmas.

Matthew was still not awake because they gave him medicine to sleep, so after we ate the oatmeal Mother sat talking with Marilyn over coffee and Ben went to open the store and I followed him out from the back.

I had only been to the store once before, in the summer, when I was very small. I caught a fish with a yellow stomach and blue eyes off the dock, but I couldn't re-member much of the store.

Now that I was older I could see things I hadn't seen when I was small and I thought how full everything looked. Full and more full.

I walked along the glass case and looked at the candy and thought how it would be fun to be in the case, just be in the case with all that candy. I wouldn't even have to eat any of it, I thought, just be with it.

Mother had told me not to ask Ben for things because of the war and how every-thing was hard to get, but Ben saw me looking at the candy and opened the back of the counter.

There was a bowl of white candy made to look like ribbons with green and red stripes in it, and he handed me one. It was colored so that the colors went all through the candy and I almost hated to eat it, but I

put it in my mouth and sucked on it and would take it out and look to make sure the colors were still there.

The candy lasted a long time because I kept taking it out and looking at it, long enough for me to go around the store and see all the things I had missed the night before and in the summer when I was so small.

I thought Ben and Marilyn must be very rich to have so many things in their store. There were boxes and boxes of food and blankets and snowshoes on the shelves, and guns hung shiny and new in racks. The head of an animal stuck so far out from the wall I could get under it.

"What is that?" I asked Ben, pointing up at the head.

"It's a moose head."

"Is it live?"

Ben was putting wood in the stove, split chunks that smelled like paint thinner, and he stopped to look at me. He smiled and shook his head. "No. They stuff them like that after they shoot them. It's full of cotton."

"Who does that?"

"The people who shoot them."

"Why do they do that?"

"So they can keep seeing it after they kill it," Ben said.

I thought, if they wanted to keep seeing it why do they kill the moose in the first place, but I didn't say it. I went the rest of the way around the store, seeing the things to see and smelling the smells that made me think of spices Mother had in our apartment in Minneapolis, and finally I came to the tree.

Standing by the tree made it seem bigger.

It went up and up to the ceiling, and the pictures in the squares on the ceiling were puffy and painted white, so they looked like clouds, and it made the tree look like it went up into the sky.

There were so many decorations. We had a tree in Minneapolis, but it was not like this tree—nothing was like this tree. There were silver balls and red balls, with dented-in sides so that they made all the light in the room seem to come out of them; and tinsel hung, each strand separate and straight, but so many that they were like water falling; and there were lights, lights that went around and around and up. While I was watching Ben plugged them in.

"Oh. . . ."

Each light had a little star around it, so when the lights came on the stars made them seem bigger and glow out in streaks of light that mixed with the streaks from the other lights.

Red and blue and yellow and green and white, all shining in the tinsel and the colored balls, so no matter where you looked there was some new light and color to see and if you lived to be forever you could not see them all. And on top, on the very top, was an angel with long white hair and a pink face and she was so beautiful, smiling down from the top of the tree, so beautiful.

"Merry Christmas," Ben said, even though it wouldn't be Christmas for two more fingers on one hand, which is how Mother had me count the days until Christmas.

"I've never seen a tree like this," I said.

"It's a special Christmas," Ben said, but his voice was breaking. When I looked at him I could see a tear, just one, come out of the corner of his left eye and run down along his nose into his beard. I couldn't see how anything as pretty as the tree could make him cry, and I was going to say that to him, but Marilyn and Mother came out of the back room.

"Come and see Matthew," Marilyn said. "He's awake and wants to see you."

They took me to Matthew's room, which was all made up like the hospital room I stayed in when I was sick and Mother thought I was going to die in a tent you could see through, except that Matthew didn't have a clear tent over his bed.

The room was all flowers and pictures of dogs and cats and pretty places on the walls, with the bed against one wall surrounded by tables and tubes and bottles and hoses.

Matthew was on the bed.

I had only seen Matthew once before, in the summer when I came up, and he didn't look different now except for his color. He was more yellow, almost as yellow as some of the lights on the tree, and so puffy-looking that it seemed if you poked him it wouldn't come back out. His eyes looked more red, and as soon as Mother and Marilyn left he waved me closer to the bed.

"I'm dying."

"I know," I said, because I did. "Except that I haven't been able to figure it out yet."

"Oh, hell, I thought it was my secret." He smiled and I saw that even his teeth seemed yellow.

"I heard Mother say it to Marilyn." I had forgotten about Matthew's swearing. He was two years older than me and had learned lots of swear words and used them all the time and was really good with them. Or bad, if you were thinking of Santa Claus. "I wasn't supposed to, but I did."

"Did they say when?"

I tried to remember and then shook my head. "No. I don't think so."

"Not too long after Christmas," he said, raising up. "Maybe in January or the next month, I can't remember the name of it." He was proud that he knew something I didn't, but it didn't make any difference, because I didn't know about months yet and was still trying to figure out how he would get to Europe so he could die and not get home.

"Now you have to tell me something," he said.

"What do you mean?"

"I told you something you didn't know—now you have to tell me something."

"We rode on the train all day yesterday to get here and I ate liver and onions that didn't taste like liver and onions—"

He shook his head. "Not like that. Not just stuff. It has to be something important —something only you know."

And of course I thought of Mr. Henderson.

"There isn't any Santa Claus," I said. "I saw Mr. Henderson in a Santa suit, only without a beard, and he was drinking red wine with his wife."

Matthew waited.

"So. That's it. I saw him, so there can't be a Santa Claus."

Matthew shook his head. "Is that all? I knew that last year and maybe even the year before—I can't be sure because the medicine they give me makes me remember things funny. But I knew it. It's just something they make up."

So I didn't have any secrets to tell Matthew like he had to tell me, especially not one where I was dying like him. But it didn't matter so much because we started to play then and we forgot secrets.

Matthew had me scout for him.

He couldn't leave the bed unless somebody was carrying him a certain way, so he would send me out in the store to see things and come back to report to him.

"Like soldiers," he said. "You report to me like a soldier."

I felt bad because I didn't have a uniform or gun or helmet like I'd seen the soldiers wearing in the newsreel when Mother took me to a Roy Rogers movie. But Matthew sent me just the same and I would sneak out to the store and watch and come back to tell Matthew what I saw.

"A fat woman bought some bread."

"An old man bought some pipe tobacco."

"Three boys came in and bought a bag of candy."

"Germans," he said. "They're all Germans and you must report to me that they're Germans."

So I did.

"A skinny German bought a little box of candy."

"Two Germans bought bottles of Coca-Cola."

Each time Matthew would salute and pretend to write down what I said on a piece of paper with a pencil, but I saw that he was just making marks. Because of the medicine he had to take, he didn't know letters any better than I did, except that he made some *A*'s that looked pretty good.

And finally, after lunch, I came in to get orders and Matthew's eyes were closed and he was asleep, and Ben said he could not play anymore until the next day because it took him down so. I couldn't see that he was down, but that's what Ben said, it took him down so.

The rest of that day I sat in the store and watched people come in and go out and ran around the aisles without knocking anything down and played under the tree until I noticed that there weren't any pack-ages under it. We had brought some presents for Marilyn and Ben and Matthew and even those weren't under the tree and I asked Ben about it.

"Santa puts them there." He was cutting meat with a slicer that he had to turn by hand and he stopped to look at me. "He puts all the presents there on Christmas Eve."

"Even ours? That we brought?"

He nodded. "All of them."

"But there isn't a Santa Claus."

"Of course there is."

"But I saw. I saw Mr. Henderson. And he doesn't live at the North Pole and he doesn't have a sled or reindeer and hates me, so there isn't a Santa Claus."

"We'll see," Ben said, smiling, only when grown-ups said that it was the same as saying nothing. Or at least it was when Mother said it. "We'll see" meant the same as "nothing."

But Ben stopped cutting meat then and gave me a bottle of 7Up, which I took to the corner by the tree to sit and drink. In the summer I had seen a plane making smoke all over the sky, and I ran in to get Mother, and she said it was a smoke writer writing the name of 7Up to make people buy it.

I watched it until the plane was all done and gone and all the smoke had blown away and saw the 7 and the *U* and the *P* and knew what they were, letters across the sky, and the same letters were on the green bottle with the girl diving and the bubbles.

I thought the green was the prettiest green in the world because you could see through it, hold it up and see through it, and I sat in the corner and looked at things through the bottle. Ben and the tree and the stove and the store and people who came to buy things from the store—looked at them all through the green bottle even

after the 7Up was gone, until it was time for dinner.

Mother and Marilyn laughed all the time when they were together, laughed so hard that Mother, and Marilyn, too, had to squat and hold herself sometimes not to pee, but they laughed while they cooked.

They cooked all the time.

I asked Mother once why she cooked so much, because sometimes she cooked at night after working all day in the laundry, made soup and cookies and cake and all so good that I would sneak and eat them when she wasn't looking, and she said, "Because your father isn't here."

Which didn't make any sense to me and wouldn't work with why Marilyn cooked, because Ben was home, not over in Europe fighting in the war, because of his feet, Mother said, but that didn't make any sense either, so I stopped asking.

They had been cooking all day and that

night for supper we had dumplings with butter on them and some soup and fresh bread and an apple pie and I ate until I couldn't move.

Matthew woke up for a little time and I went in to sit with him, but the medicine made him not talk or see right, so it wasn't the same as the afternoon and in a little while Mother pulled the couch out and I went to bed.

She and Ben and Marilyn sat at the kitchen table and drank coffee and talked, and their words all mixed until it was like a song and I was almost asleep when I heard them say Santa Claus and Matthew, but nothing else. Nothing that made sense because by then I was dreaming of Father and Europe, and wondering if when Matthew died would he be with Father if Father died, and could I go and see them?

.   .   .

Christmas Eve day.

In the morning Mother and Marilyn made cinnamon rolls and I got to eat two of them before I went in to play with Matthew.

But he wasn't feeling very well and was more yellow than he'd been the day before, so we didn't scout or report, but just sat and looked at magazines and picture books and worked in some coloring books except that I couldn't stay in the lines so well and he made fun of me.

But after a little time he put his coloring book down and looked at me and was crying.

"What's wrong?"

"I don't want to die."

"It won't be so bad." I was coloring a pig jumping in flowers and I put my crayon down. "Mother says it just means you go to sleep and don't come home from Europe."

"I still don't want to die."

He turned away from me and faced the wall and I thought it was wrong for him to be sad on Christmas Eve day, so I made a face with my fingers in my mouth, and when that didn't work I said, "Maybe I was wrong and there is a Santa Claus and he'll come and bring us lots of presents—"

"Oh, hell, there isn't any old Santa Claus."

And I turned and saw that Ben had been coming through the door and had heard it, all of it, and that his face was white and his eyes pinched and he wiped his nose and coughed.

"Maybe he's right," Ben said to Matthew, but his voice was scratchy and he was having trouble talking. "Maybe there is a Santa and he'll come and bring wonderful things, wonderful things, wonderful things. . . ."

He rubbed his hand on Matthew's cheek and pushed his hair back the way

Mother pushed my hair back sometimes, the same touch, and I thought how white and red Ben's skin looked where his hand touched Matthew against the yellow. How white and clean. And then I thought how they were the same, how Ben looked at Matthew the way Mother looked at me when I was in the clear tent in the hospital and the minister was there and how soft that look was, how soft his touch was, and saw that Ben was crying. I sat with the picture of the pig on my lap and wondered why everybody felt so bad.

And even when Ben left and I stayed and Matthew started to color again it wasn't the same as before. Something was gone.

Gone from him.

I said let's play Germans and he said no.

I said let's make faces and he said no.

Whatever I said, he said no and then he

looked at me and swore, a really good word, and said, "Santa is just a big old fat liar."

I stared at him.

"He says he's something and he'll come, but it's all a big lie and he's a big old fat liar."

It was too much to say at once. Even if Santa turned out not to be real, it was too dangerous to say all that on the night before Christmas day. "But we don't know . . ." And I was going to say we don't know anything about him, about any of it, but it didn't come out.

"He won't come. He won't come. He won't come."

And he swore some more, but I had covered my ears and hoped that nobody had heard, and when he turned to the wall again I left the room and went to where Mother was sitting at the table talking to

Marilyn and leaned against her leg and put my head on her arm.

"What's the matter, punkin? Don't you feel good?"

"I'm okay."

"Did Matthew go back to sleep?"

"Sort of." I thought for a little time and then I asked, "If there isn't a Santa Claus, do you still have to be good like if there is a Santa Claus?"

"Don't worry about it—there is a Santa Claus if you want there to be a Santa Claus."

"There is?"

She nodded. "That's how it works. If you think hard about it and want it enough there will be a Santa."

I went back into Matthew's room and sat by his bed. For a minute I thought he had gone to sleep and I looked at my coloring book and the picture of the pig and then Matthew moved.

"You're back."

"Mother says it's up to us if there's a Santa Claus or not."

"What do you mean?"

"She says if we want him, if we want him hard enough, there will be a Santa; and if we don't want him there won't be one."

He didn't say anything for a long time, and I thought he was thinking of something smart to say and that maybe he was going to swear. I thought if he swore about Mother I would leave the room again and not come back, and I didn't care if he was sick and dying or not, but he didn't.

He didn't say anything about Mother, and he didn't swear.

He looked at me, right into my eyes, and he said, "I want him to be."

And I said, "I want him to be too."

And he said, "No. I mean I want him to be, more than anything else in the whole world, more than all the things I've ever wanted, more than I want to live, I want him to be."

And his voice was soft and hissing and I knew he meant it, meant it really; and I meant it, too, only maybe not as strong as Matthew, and it scared me. The tight part of how he looked scared me because I didn't know how that could be, how that look could be.

"Let's think all day," he said. "Let's think there is a Santa all day and maybe it will be and he will come."

So we thought it all day and when I would not be thinking it Matthew would remind me and when he was not thinking of it I would remind him until it was late afternoon and Matthew took his medicine and could not think right anymore and turned to face the wall. But he kept saying right along, until the words rolled into each other:

"Think it, think it, think it . . ."

And I went back into the kitchen to watch Mother and Marilyn cook. They were making *lefse,* cooking the big flat pieces of dough on the griddle on the stove and Mother sprinkled sugar on one and rolled it up and let me eat it.

"It tastes like potatoes with sugar on them," I said, and she laughed.

"That's because they're made out of potato flour."

"We have been thinking about Santa all afternoon," I said. "Matthew and me. And we thought hard that he was real. Do you think it was enough?"

She smiled at Marilyn and then down at me. "If you thought it right, then he is real."

"And he'll come? He'll come and find us and bring presents?"

"If you were good."

But it was such a long time to wait. All that afternoon and all that night. Such a long time that I started to think wrong again and remembered Mr. Henderson and the wine and thought it didn't matter what I thought—Mr. Henderson had been there and there must not be a Santa Claus and it was all just grown-up talk about believing in him.

I went out by the tree where there were still no presents and sat looking up at the angel with the white hair and thought of Santa, but it only made me sad. I could not think of Santa without thinking of Matthew and how it would be sad for him that there wasn't a Santa when he didn't come home from Europe, when he died—he would never have seen Santa because there wasn't a Santa.

And finally it was dark.

Outside the store windows it was dark, and Ben turned off the main store lights, so the tree seemed to grow, the lights seemed to grow and was so pretty it was hard to breathe, just looking at it. I went into the kitchen and took Mother's hand to come and see the tree and she followed me out.

"See the angel," I said, pointing. "Doesn't she have pretty hair?"

Mother nodded and picked me up and hugged me, and Ben and Marilyn came out of the apartment then, pulling the couch.

"Help us," they said, and we moved the table and chairs out into the store by the tree.

Ben set the table and Marilyn and Mother brought food and I brought a lamp out and put it on the table. When it was done and ready, Ben carried Matthew out and put him in blankets on the couch. The little sleep had made the medicine wear off, and he smiled at us.

Then we ate some soup with dumplings, and potato sausage that made me burp, and some smelly fish called *lutefisk* that I had never tasted before and would

not want to taste again, and some dough folded over something sweet, and milk.

We ate and ate by the tree with the angel looking down, and when we were done Ben sat on the couch by Matthew's feet and Mother and I sat on the floor and the stove was warm and it was hard to stay awake. But Ben opened a book and read a poem about Santa Claus and the night before Christmas, and I looked at Matthew, who listened to each word of the book, every and each word; and so did I, and I thought, it didn't matter.

It didn't matter if there was a Santa Claus or there wasn't a Santa Claus. It would not make the food different or the tree different or the angel different or how it felt to lean against Mother and listen to the story as it named the reindeer and told how they came in the night. I looked at Matthew, who was seeing them the way I was seeing them all.

In the tree.

When it was done and Ben closed the book because all the words had been said and all the pictures had been seen and it was time to close the book we all sat quietly, just sat and felt the heat from the stove. I thought of Christmas and how it was and what it must be like in the war for Father, and hoped he had a tree and somebody to read to him out of a book.

"Merry Christmas," Matthew said in a whisper to me, and I shook my head.

"It's not Christmas yet. We have to go to bed and wait and then it will be Christmas."

But we didn't go to bed, even though it was late and warm and we were sleepy. I saw that Matthew's eyes were closing and I couldn't keep my eyes open either and closed them, closed them just a little.

"What's that?"

Ben stood up and I didn't know if I

was asleep or not, but I opened my eyes and Matthew did the same and I felt Mother move next to me.

"What?" Matthew asked.

"I thought I heard bells," Ben said, holding up his hand. "Outside. I thought I heard sleigh bells."

And he made the face grown-ups make when they are making things up so they think you'll believe them, and Matthew looked at me and I saw he didn't believe it either.

"No. Listen."

And I heard them. Heard the bells. Ringing low, and somehow coming from all around.

"Let's see, let's see. . . ."

Ben motioned with his hands and picked Matthew up, wrapped in his blankets, and we all followed him through the store to the front door, where he stood aside and let Marilyn open it.

Cold air came in along the floor and I went up next to Ben's legs and looked out.

I didn't see anything at first. There was a moon that made all the snow white, and the moonlight mixed with the light coming from the front of the store to make puddles of light places on the snow, but I didn't see anything.

Then something moved.

"What—"

I heard Matthew. He was higher than me because Ben was holding him up and he could see better, and I heard him start to say something and then nothing. Just his breath sucking in.

But something moved and I heard the bells again and it came then, came into the moonlight and store light, into the puddles of light, and I saw it as plain as anything.

It was a reindeer and then another reindeer and two more, and they were walking, and they had harnesses on and they were pulling a sleigh and it came, too, came with them and pulled up right in front of the door.

Right there.

Right there in front of the store. And I know they weren't flying and I know there weren't a whole bunch of them, but there were four and they pulled the sleigh and it stopped, stopped there in front of the door and there he sat in the sleigh.

Santa Claus.

With his white beard and red suit and hat, he sat in the sleigh; with his glasses and big stomach and bag of toys, he sat in the sleigh and looked at us and smiled.

Santa Claus.

And I was so scared I stopped breathing.

"It's him," I thought I heard somebody say, but it was me, and I said it like I was talking to the angel at the top of the tree.

"Touch it."

It was Matthew, and he was talking to me and I knew it, but I couldn't move. The grown-ups stood and watched and I thought it was funny because they were watching us and not Santa and I couldn't move. "What?"

"Go touch it. Make sure it's real."

His voice was soft the way it had been in the room when we were thinking of Santa and he had wanted it so much, and I heard it and my feet moved.

They moved me out the door, and I hated them because the other parts of me didn't want to move, but they moved me and I walked across the snow by the door and to the first reindeer and looked up and it was real.

The antlers crossed the moon the way Mother said the smoke from the little houses on the lake crossed the moon, went up and up to the moon, and they were real and his eye was so big I could see myself in it, big and brown and round, and there I was, standing next to him.

He shook his head and the antlers moved in big swings and I turned to run, but Matthew was looking at me.

"*Touch* it!"

So I did.

I reached out and touched the reindeer on the leg and felt the hair, the warm hair, and the leg moved and I turned to Matthew and said, "It's real."

"For *real* real?"

"For real."

"Pull his beard."

"What?"

"Get into the sleigh and pull his beard."

And I would not, could not have been able to do that except that my legs moved, kept moving, and I walked past the reindeer and to the sleigh and looked up and knew he was real, *knew* he was real and he smiled and I stood on the side of the sleigh and touched his beard, pulled on it.

And it was real.

"It's real."

"For *real* real?"

"Real."

"It's him." His voice was soft, a whisper.

"Yes. It's him."

And I jumped down and ran then, ran

to stand with Mother, and we stood away
from the door and watched him come in
with his sack, come right in the door and
put presents all around under the tree until
the sack was empty and the tree was full.
Then he turned and looked at us, looked at
Matthew, and still without saying a word
went out of the door and we watched him
move away into the darkness, the reindeer
trotting and the bells jingling softly until we
could not see him or the sleigh or the deer,

could not hear him and Matthew sighed once more and said, "It's him."

And it was him.

It was him for that Christmas and all the Christmases since; it was him later when Matthew did not come home again and I went to the funeral and tried to tell Mother he was just sleeping and not to cry; it was him when Father did come home from Europe and we had Christmases together; it was him for each and every Christmas of each and every year that I have lived since then, and will still be him for each and every Christmas of each and every year that I have yet remaining.

It was him.

Don't miss *Brian's Winter,*
a companion novel to
The River and *Hatchet*

BRIAN'S WINTER
GARY PAULSEN

ISBN: 0-385-32198-8

In Gary Paulsen's classic novel *Hatchet,*
thirteen-year-old Brian Robeson is stranded in
the Canadian wilderness. To survive, he must
rely on his intelligence, his instincts, and one
tool: a hatchet. Finally, as millions of readers
know, he is rescued at the end of the summer.

But what if Brian *hadn't* been rescued? What if
Brian had been left to confront his deadliest
enemy—winter?

Find out in *Brian's Winter.*

On sale now from Delacorte Press!